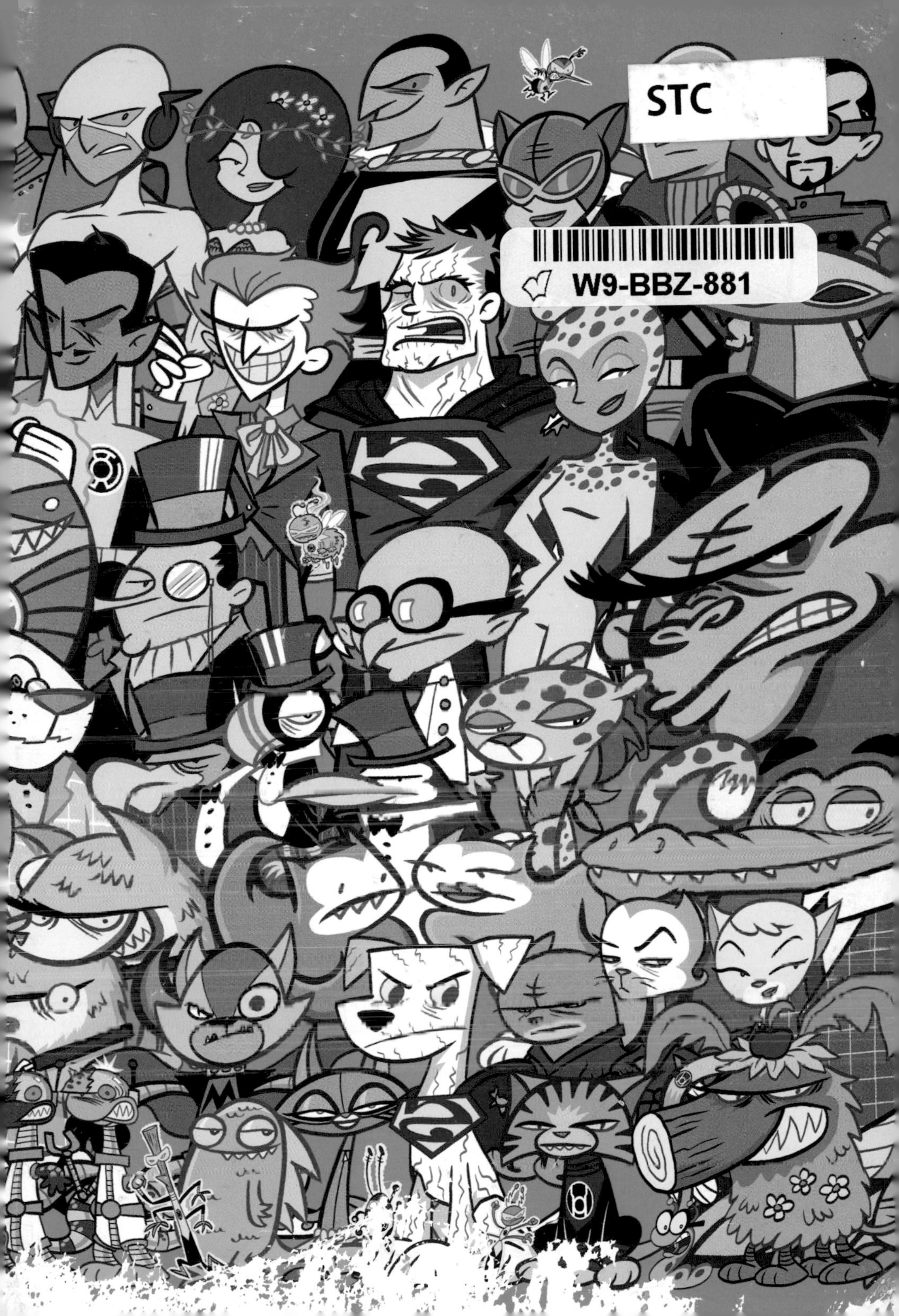

DC™ SUPER-PETS!

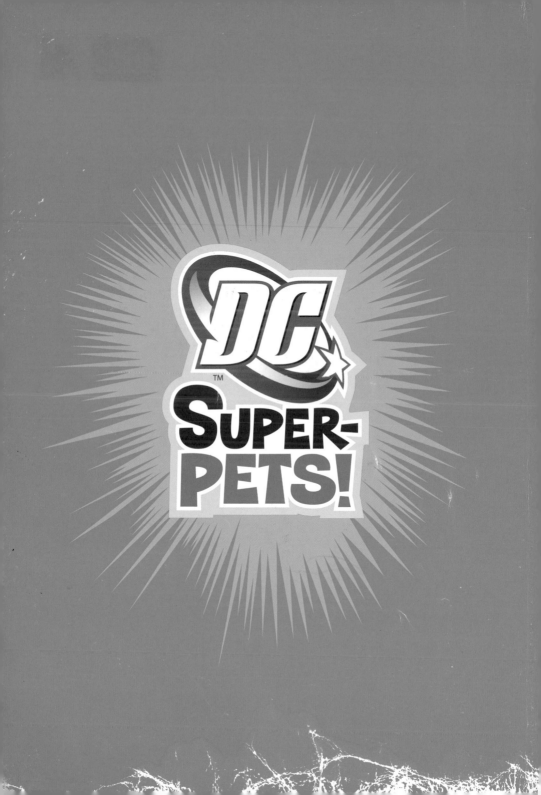

by John
Sazaklis

SALAMANDER SMACK DOWN

illustrated by
Art Baltazar

Picture Window Books™
a capstone imprint

Starring...

X-43
THE CYBORG NEWT!

WHATZIT
THE TERRIFIC TURTLE!

BIT-BIT
ALSO A CYBORG NEWT!

PROFESSOR ZOOM
THE REVERSE FLASH!

TABLE OF CONTENTS!

Central City Police DATABASE

SUPER-PET HERO FILE 006:
WHATZIT

Quick Wits

Speedy Reflexes

Sleek Uniform

Super-speed

Super Hero Owner:
THE FLASH

Species: Turtle

Place of Birth: Zooville

Age: Unknown

Favorite Food: Shellfish

Bio: Merton McSnurtle has followed in the lightning-fast footsteps of the World's Greatest Speedsters, including his current owner, Barry Allen.

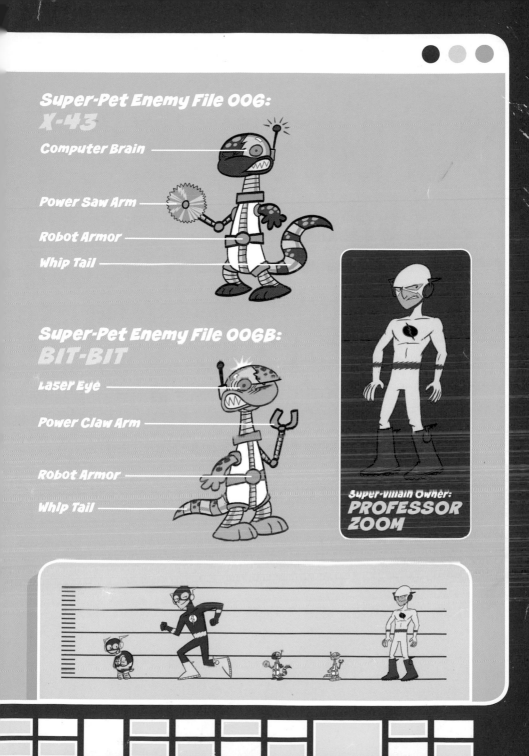

Super-Pet Enemy File 006:
X-43

Computer Brain

Power Saw Arm

Robot Armor

Whip Tail

Super-Pet Enemy File 006B:
BIT-BIT

Laser Eye

Power Claw Arm

Robot Armor

Whip Tail

Super-villain Owner:
PROFESSOR ZOOM

TURTLE POWER

It was a beautiful morning in Central City. **Merton McSnurtle** strolled slowly through his favorite park.

Of course, Merton was only acting slow because he was a turtle. Those are the rules. Even his friends didn't know Merton's little secret.

He was **Flash's** speedy Super-Pet. When trouble was near, he became the Fastest Turtle on Earth, the **Terrific Whatzit.**

Across the street, a large truck headed toward a farmer's market.

Suddenly, the truck's front tire blew.

KA-POW!

The pickup truck jerked forward. Its shipment of wooden crates broke open and flew into the air. A shower of freshly laid eggs filled the sky.

Uh-oh! thought Merton. **That's going to be one very big omelet!**

With blinding speed, Merton changed into the Terrific Whatzit. He zoomed toward the truck. Zigging and zagging, Whatzit snatched every egg from the air.

FWIP! FWIP! FWIP!

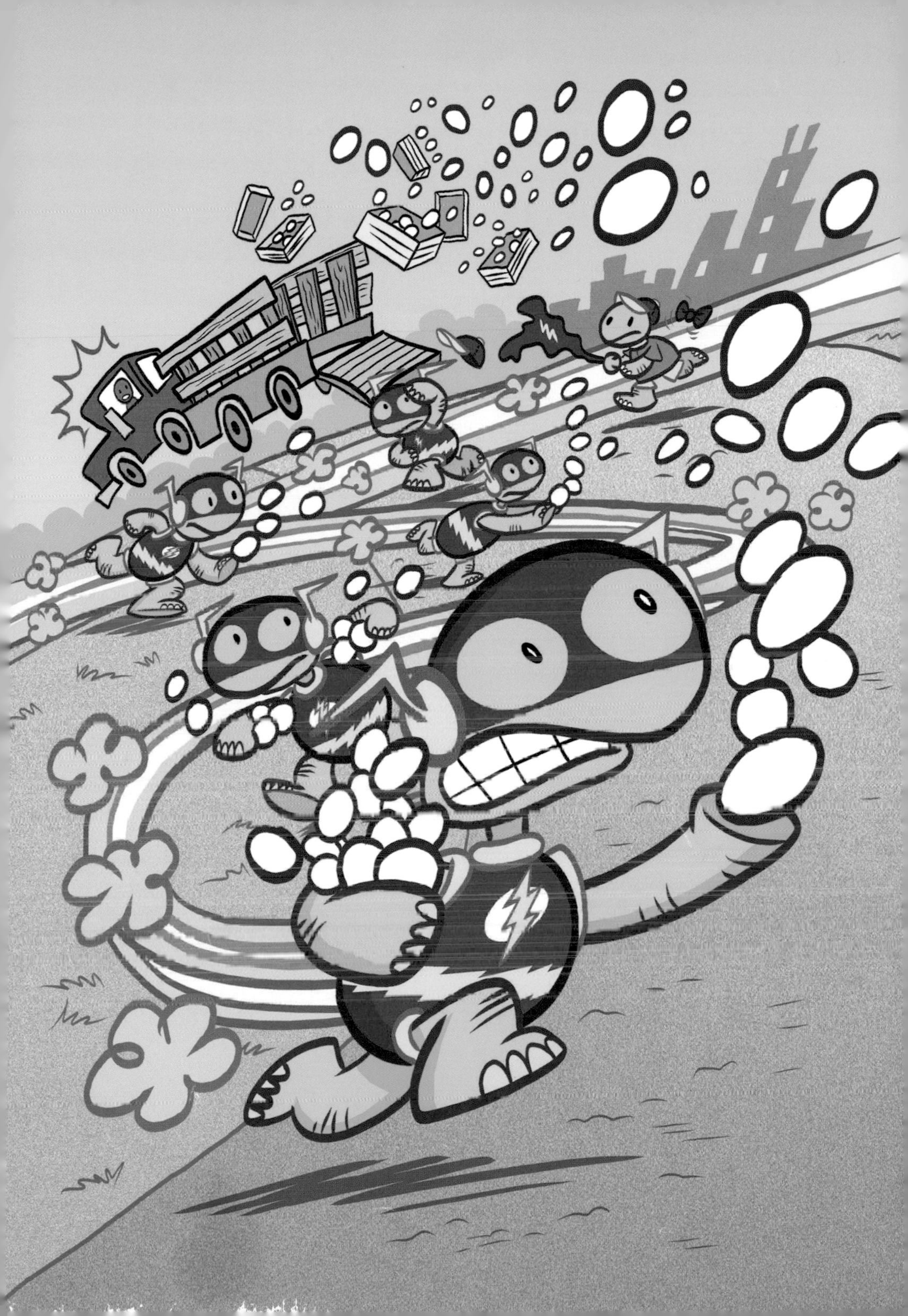

Whatzit piled the eggs safely back into the crates. Then he set them gently on the sidewalk.

Seconds passed, but the trouble was far from over. Whatzit sped ahead of the truck and stopped in front of it. He spun his arms faster and faster.

WHOOSH!

The hero formed two whirlwinds that pushed against the out-of-control vehicle. The truck slowed to a stop inches away from Whatzit's nose.

Behind the wheel, the driver wiped his forehead. He breathed a sigh of relief. "Whew! Thank you," said the driver.

"Don't sweat it!" Whatzit replied. **"I love being a speedy turtle!"**

Around him, the crowd from the park cheered. "Hip, hip, hooray!"

Pets and owners clapped their hands and paws and wings with excitement. **The hero smiled and took a bow.**

* * *

Of course, not all of Central City cared for their heroes. There was a part of town where no-good people went about their no-good business. It's there one would find the E. Vill Pet Store. A man named Edgar Vill, who raised pets for super-villains, ran the shop.

Inside this pet store, by the front window, there was a glass tank with two cyborg newts inside. Their names were **X-43**, a purple-spotted newt, and **Bit-Bit**, a paddle-tailed newt. X-43 was quick and smart. Bit-Bit was big and strong, but not very bright.

CYBORG
NEWTS
99¢ EACH

A sinister man passed by the pet

store as the newts watched. He was

tall and wore glasses. He had a leather

satchel over his shoulder.

X-43 pressed his little webbed hands

against the glass.

"Bit-Bit, wake up! Do you know who that is?" cried the clever newt.

Bit-Bit opened one eye and sniffed around. **"Is it lunchtime yet?"** he asked.

"That is **Professor Zoom!** He is the Flash's enemy and an evil genius," X-43 said. "The man is my idol!"

"Hahaha! That's a cool name," Bit-Bit said. **"Zoom, zoom, zoom!"** He repeated the words and lazily waved his tail around.

"Bit-Bit, you're a nitwit!" X-43

shouted. He climbed to the top of the

cage. "This is my chance to prove

myself as a criminal mastermind. Now

move it!"

The lazy newt followed his leader.

Together, they squeezed under the pet

shop door. They soon caught up to

Professor Zoom.

Bit-Bit lifted X-43 onto his back and

leaped into the villain's satchel. X-43

could barely contain his joy!

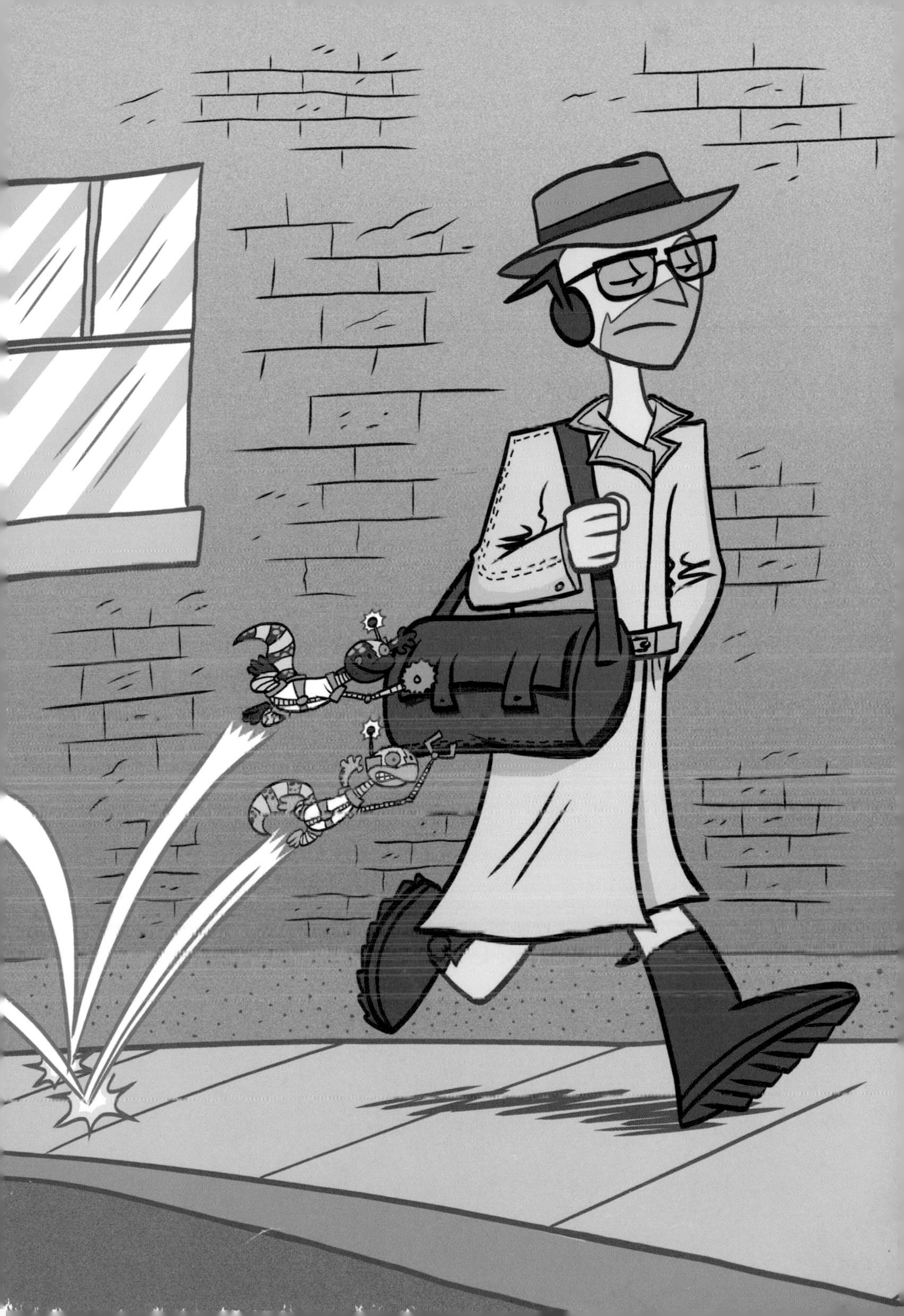

NAUGHTY NEWTS

The trip inside the satchel was bumpy and dark. A long while passed. Finally, there was a heavy thud and the closing of a door.

X-43 peeked his head out of the bag. All around them were shiny metal tables, shelves, tools, and machines.

"**Amazing!**" X-43 gasped. "We are in Professor Zoom's secret lab. This is where the madness happens!"

Near the back wall was a large machine. X-43 nudged Bit-Bit. He had been napping during the entire trip. The lazy newt opened his eyes slowly. He asked if there was anything to eat.

THWAP!

X-43 slapped Bit-Bit with his tail. Then the newts scurried off the table and toward the other end of the lab.

Soon, a giant machine came into full view. It stood two stories tall and looked like the Flash. The colors of his costume had been reversed. The main part was yellow. A red lightning bolt scarred a black circle on the chest, forming a fearful symbol.

"This is incredible," X-43 said. **"Why haven't we seen this robot in action?"**

The evil newt made his way onto the table near the robot's foot. Scattered across the top were several blueprints and handwritten notes.

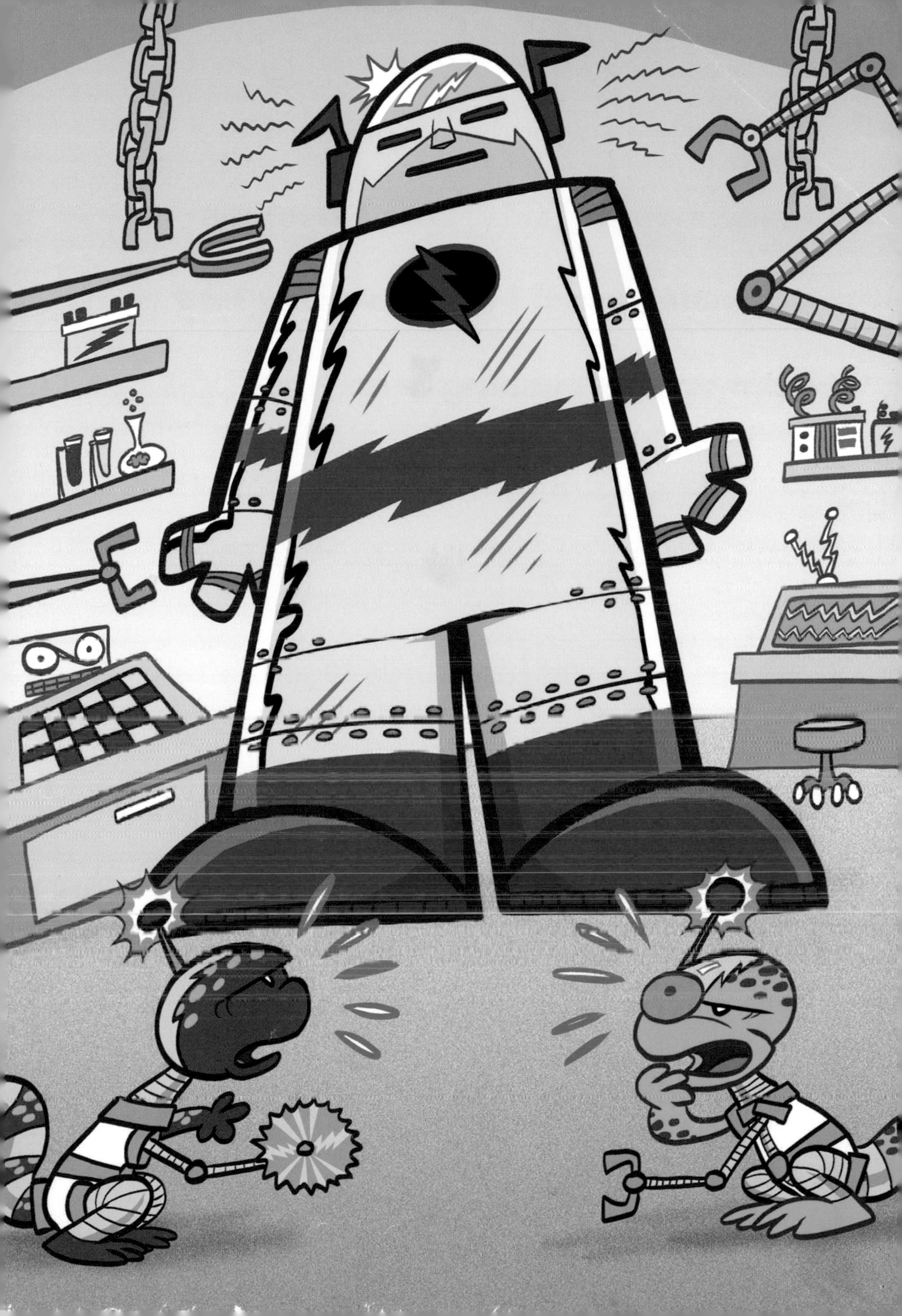

"Well, no wonder," X-43 said, shaking his head. **"These designs are all wrong! I can have this bad bot up and running in no time."**

"Hey, X," Bit-Bit called up from the floor. "When do we eat?"

X-43 rubbed his hands together and grinned. "First, we'll scare the town with this giant robot," he said. "Then, Professor Zoom will ask me to join his criminal crusade, and you will be able to eat this monster's weight in sweets. Central City will be ours!"

Bit-Bit liked the sound of that. He got to work helping X-43 bring the Reverse Flash robot to life.

Once they were finished, the newts climbed up the robot. They entered the cockpit inside its head.

Along the control panel were four levers. Each one controlled an arm and a leg. X-43 took a deep breath and hopped onto the red power button.

Before he pressed down, Bit-Bit stopped him.

"We need a name for our robot," Bit-Bit said.

X-43 glared at him and spoke through gritted teeth. **"What did you have in mind?"** he asked.

"How about Speedy?" replied Bit-Bit.

"I don't think so," said X-43.

"Zoom-Zoom," Bit-Bit suggested.

"Negative."

"Ok, um . . . Revvy?" added Bit-Bit.

"I like it," exclaimed X-43. **"Now let's go!"**

The naughty newt pushed the red
button. Electricity buzzed through the
massive mechanical man.

The eye sockets lit up. Revvy was
ready to rumble!

Meanwhile, **Merton McSnurtle** was sitting at an outdoor diner. He just finished his fifth afternoon milkshake in only four minutes. Merton swirled the straw inside the empty glass. He tapped his foot.

Time sure moves slowly around here when there's nothing to do, he thought. *If only there was some action, some excitement, even a little danger!*

Suddenly, a screaming crowd came running out of the town square.

"Help! Danger!" they yelled, pushing

past the turtle.

"Finally!" Merton cheered, hopping

out of his seat.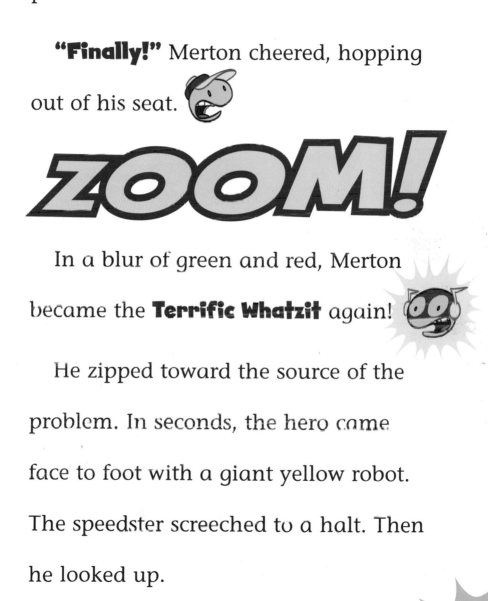

ZOOM!

In a blur of green and red, Merton

became the **Terrific Whatzit** again!

He zipped toward the source of the

problem. In seconds, the hero came

face to foot with a giant yellow robot.

The speedster screeched to a halt. Then

he looked up.

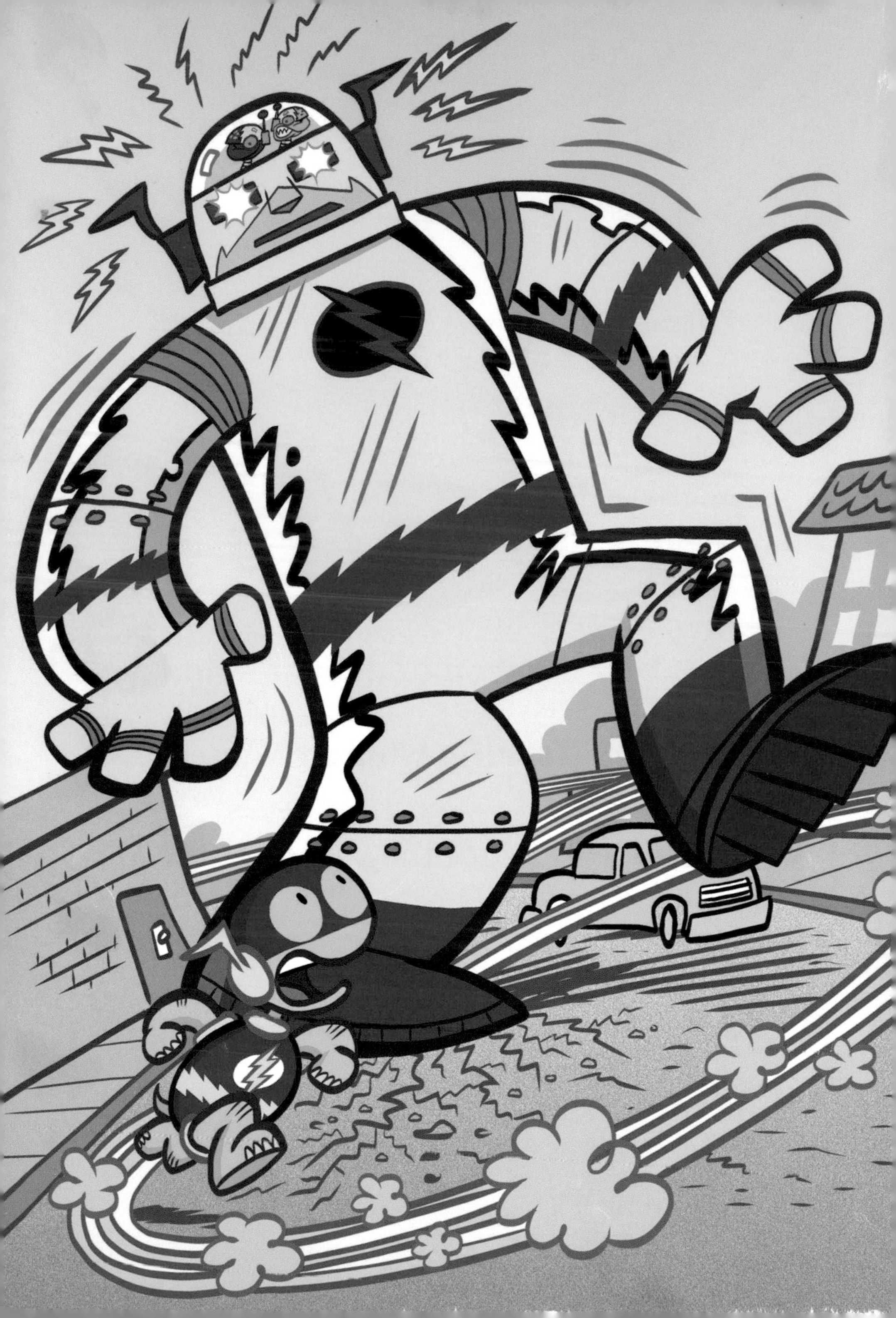

"Who are you?" Whatzit wondered aloud. **"What do you want?"**

X-43 spoke into a microphone. A voice boomed out of Revvy's head.

"I am X-43," said the newt. "And I want this city to fear me. Know my name! Know that I am a force to be reckoned with!"

"I reckon you're off your rocker," Whatzit said and laughed. "Now why don't we put this giant evil robot back inside its giant evil toybox?"

"You ridiculous reptile!" X-43 yelled. "I'm going to make turtle soup out of you!"

With that, the nasty newt pushed one of the buttons with all his might. Revvy's left foot lifted high in the air. Then it came crashing down.

KA-BLAMO!

Whatzit zoomed out of the way.

There was now a large crater where

the hero once stood. Whatzit appeared

behind the robot.

"You missed," Whatzit said.

X-43 ordered Bit-Bit to push a
different button. The robot's right foot
came crashing down, and Whatzit
disappeared again. Revvy continued to
stomp. Left foot, right foot. Left, right.

CRASH! BOOM! BANG!

Whatzit weaved between the robot's legs. "Nice moves, big guy," the hero said with a chuckle. **"You dance like you have two lead feet!"**

Then everything went black. A metal fist clamped shut around Whatzit's body. X-43 pulled a lever, tightening the robot's grip.

"Looks like someone's a little shell-shocked," X-43 joked to Bit-Bit.

The hero's shell was super-strong. Unfortunately, Revvy's grip was too tight for Whatzit to breathe. Soon, he was going to run out of air.

Whatzit needed to come up with an escape plan . . . **and fast!**

Chapter 3

SHELL SHOCKED

The Terrific Whatzit was in a terrible bind. The lack of air was making his head spin, but that gave him an idea!

Whatzit focused all his energy. He started to shake in place. Soon, his body broke into a million little pieces.

The itty-bitty pieces easily passed

through the robot's giant metal fist.

Moments later, the pieces stuck back

together. They took the shape of

Whatzit once again.

   "Phew!" the hero said with a deep

breath. **"Now it's time to put an end**

to this robot rampage!"

   Whatzit rushed toward Revvy's head.

He found a way in through the robot's

nose. He hurried into the large nostril.

THUNK! Whatzit was stuck!

The hero's shell was too wide to get through. The daring escape had tired Whatzit. He wasn't strong enough to shake apart again.

X-43 looked through the robot's glass dome. **He saw two little green legs dangling out of Revvy's nose.**

X-43 pushed a few gears and pulled a few levers. The robot's left hand came up to the nose. Its metal fingers tried to pick Whatzit out!

Thinking fast, Whatzit wriggled and squirmed until he popped out of his shell. He landed forcefully inside the control panel. Standing between the newts was a shell-less green creature in shiny red tights.

"What's that?" Bit-Bit asked.

"It's Whatzit!" yelled X-43. "Get him, you fool!"

FWOOSH!

Bit-Bit leaped at the speedster, but

caught nothing but air!

Whatzit stood in front of the control panel with his hands on his hips. Bit-Bit snorted. He charged at the hero once again.

Whatzit flipped out of the way, and the newt brute slammed into a lever. The robot's right fist lifted up and punched its own head. The glass in the right eye socket shattered. Revvy spiraled out of control, heading into a row of power lines.

"Let's get out of here," Whatzit said and grabbed the newts.

In a flash, the hero slid down the robot's nostril. He popped into his shell again and zoomed to safety.

The three of them watched as Revvy stumbled into the electric wires.

ZAAAP!!!

A surge of power short-circuited the monstrous machine, shutting it down. The villainous vehicle towered silently over the town square. It was no longer a threat to the good citizens or their fair city.

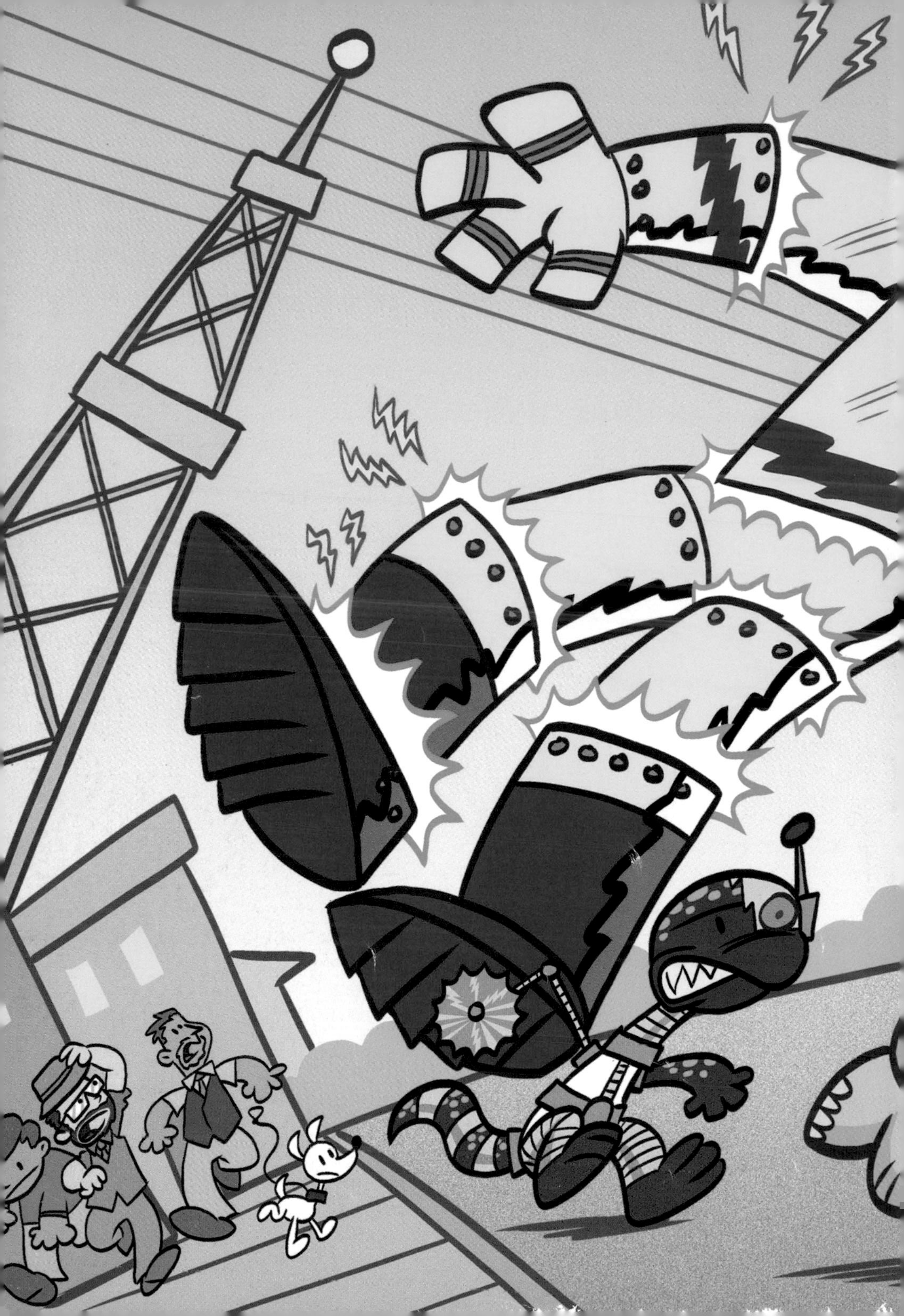

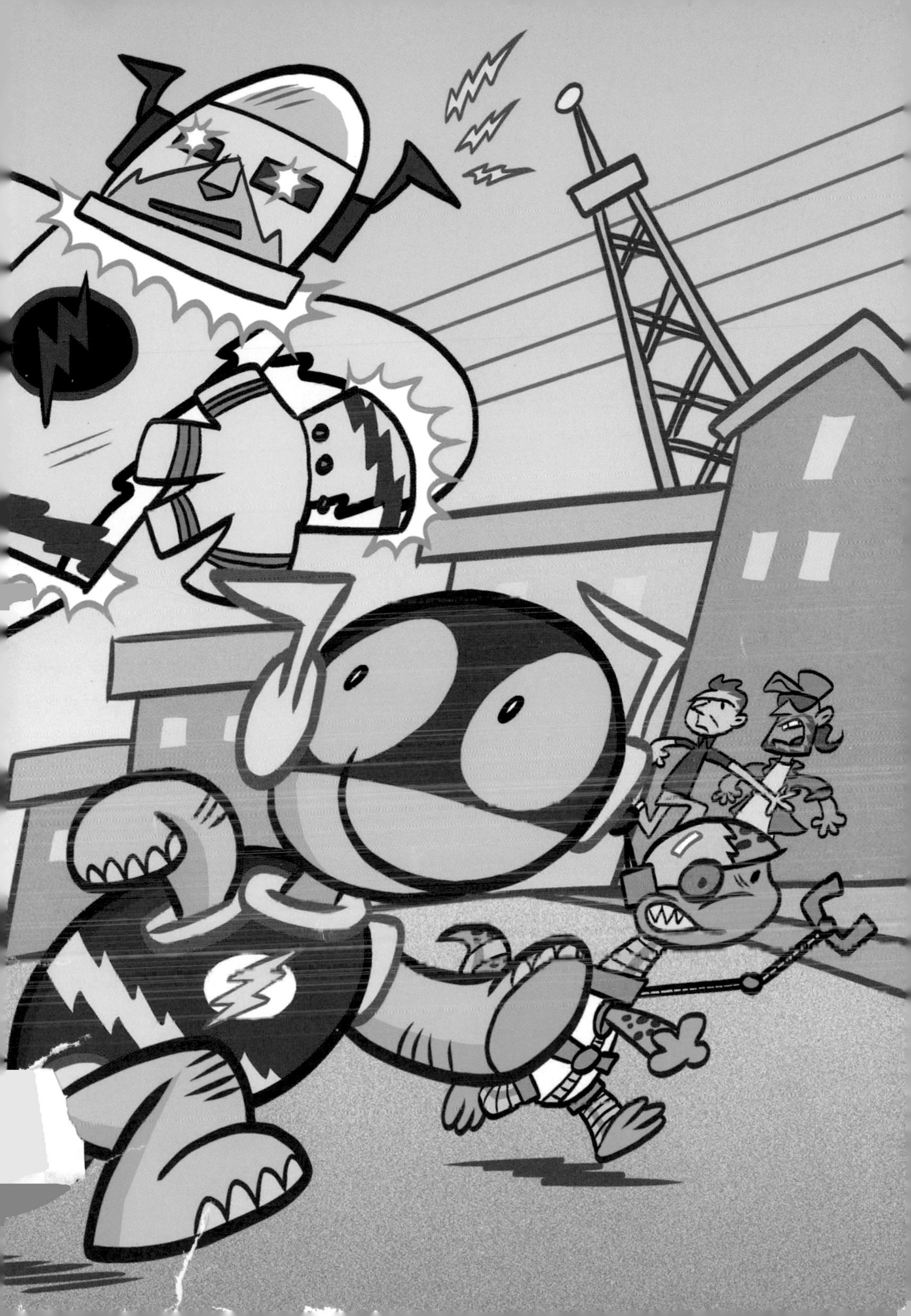

"Stop right there, you slimy

salamanders!" shouted Whatzit.

"I'm not a salamander," replied Bit-

Bit. **"I'm a newt!"**

"Bit-Bit, you nitwit," said X-43.

"Newts ARE salamanders!"

Whatzit quickly caught the newts. He

tied their tails together. X-43 and Bit-Bit

ran in opposite directions only to snap

back and knock each other out.

Whatzit took this opportunity to take apart the robot. He began running around Revvy, faster and faster. He created a cyclone of air.

The robot lifted off the ground as its joints began to rattle. First the screws flew out. Then the pieces collapsed into a giant heap of scrap metal.

Whatzit climbed atop the pile. He struck a heroic pose for the arriving news teams and camera crews. People returned to the square. They congratulated their hero.

A short time later, animal control arrived. They took the sneaky salamanders back to the pet shop where they belonged. **The Terrific Whatzit had restored peace and safety to Central City . . . for now.**

* * *

The next day, at the E. Vill Pet Store, X-43 and Bit-Bit watched the news on TV. The city's mayor was rewarding Whatzit with a medal.

The ceremony was taking place inside a museum. The busted robot had become part of the display.

"Bah!" yelled X-43. He stormed to the opposite end of the glass tank. "We could've made Professor Zoom proud and become part of his team. Instead, we're stuck back here!"

"**Aw, it's not so bad,**" Bit-Bit said

between mouthfuls of food.

Suddenly, a man entered the store.

He walked to the newt tank.

"Mr. Vill, I'd like to adopt these

amazing creatures," said the man.

X-43 looked up to see . . . **Professor**

Zoom! The newt hopped out of the

tank into the waiting hand of his idol.

"Are you the ones who got my

robot to work?" Zoom asked.

X-43 and Bit-Bit nodded.

"Welcome to the family, boys," said the professor.

X-43 smiled. He would finally get a chance to work with his evil idol.

Then Zoom added, **"You'll make perfect pets for my brat of a nephew!"**

KNOW YOUR HERO PETS!

1. Krypto
2. Streaky
3. Beppo
4. Comet
5. Ace
6. Robin Robin
7. Jumpa
8. Whatzit
9. Storm
10. Topo
11. Ark
12. Hoppy
13. Batcow
14. Big Ted
15. Proty
16. Gleek
17. Paw Pooch
18. Bull Dog
19. Chameleon Collie
20. Hot Dog
21. Tail Terrier
22. Tusky Husky
23. Mammoth Mutt
24. Dawg
25. B'dg
26. Stripezoid
27. Zallion
28. Ribitz
29. Bzzd
30. Gratch
31. Buzzoo
32. Fossfur
33. Zhoomp
34. Eeny

KNOW YOUR VILLAIN PETS!

1. Bizarro Krypto
2. Ignatius
3. Rozz
4. Mechanikat
5. Crackers
6. Giggles
7. Joker Fish
8. Chauncey
9. Artie Puffin
10. Griff
11. Waddles
12. Dogwood
13. Mr. Mind
14. Sobek
15. Misty
16. Sneezers
17. General Manx
18. Nizz
19. Fer-El
20. Titano
21. Bit-Bit
22. X-43
23. Dex-Starr
24. Glomulus
25. Whoosh
26. Pronto
27. Snorrt
28. Rolf
29. Tootz
30. Eezix
31. Donald
32. Waxxee
33. Fimble
34. Webbik

AW YEAH, JOKES!

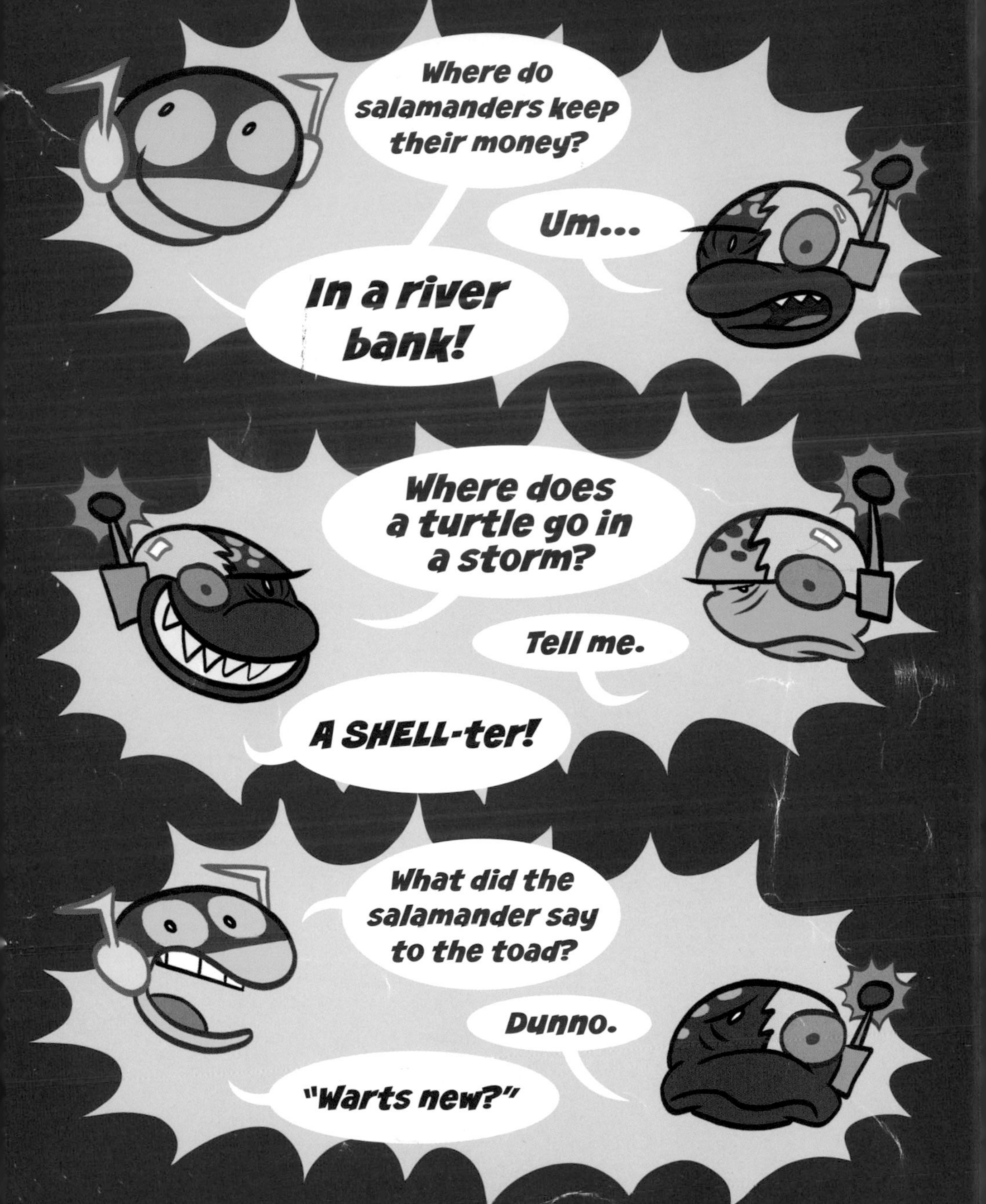
Where do salamanders keep their money?
Um...
In a river bank!
Where does a turtle go in a storm?
Tell me.
A SHELL-ter!
What did the salamander say to the toad?
Dunno.
"Warts new?"

WORD POWER!

cyclone (SYE-klone)—another name for a tornado, a storm with very strong winds

idol (EYE-duhl)—someone loved and admired

mastermind (MASS-tur-minde)—the person (or animal) controlling the way a plan is carried out

newt (NOOT)—a salamander with short legs and a long tail that lives on land but lays eggs in the water

omelet (OM-lit)—eggs that have been beaten, cooked in a pan, and folded over with ingredients inside

satchel (SACH-uhl)—a bag carried over the shoulder

sinister (SIN-uh-stur)—evil and threatening

MEET THE AUTHOR!

John Sazaklis

John Sazaklis spent part of life working in a family coffee shop, the House of Donuts. The other part, he spent drawing and writing stories. He has illustrated Spider-Man books and written Batman books for HarperCollins. John lives in the Big Apple and takes a bite out of it every day.

MEET THE ILLUSTRATOR!

Eisner Award-winner Art Baltazar

Art Baltazar is a cartoonist machine from the heart of Chicago! He defines cartoons and comics not only as an art style, but as a way of life. Currently, Art is the creative force behind *The New York Times* best-selling, Eisner Award-winning, DC Comics series Tiny Titans, and the co-writer for *Billy Batson and the Magic of SHAZAM!* Art is living the dream! He draws comics and never has to leave the house. He lives with his lovely wife, Rose, big boy Sonny, little boy Gordon, and little girl Audrey. Right on!

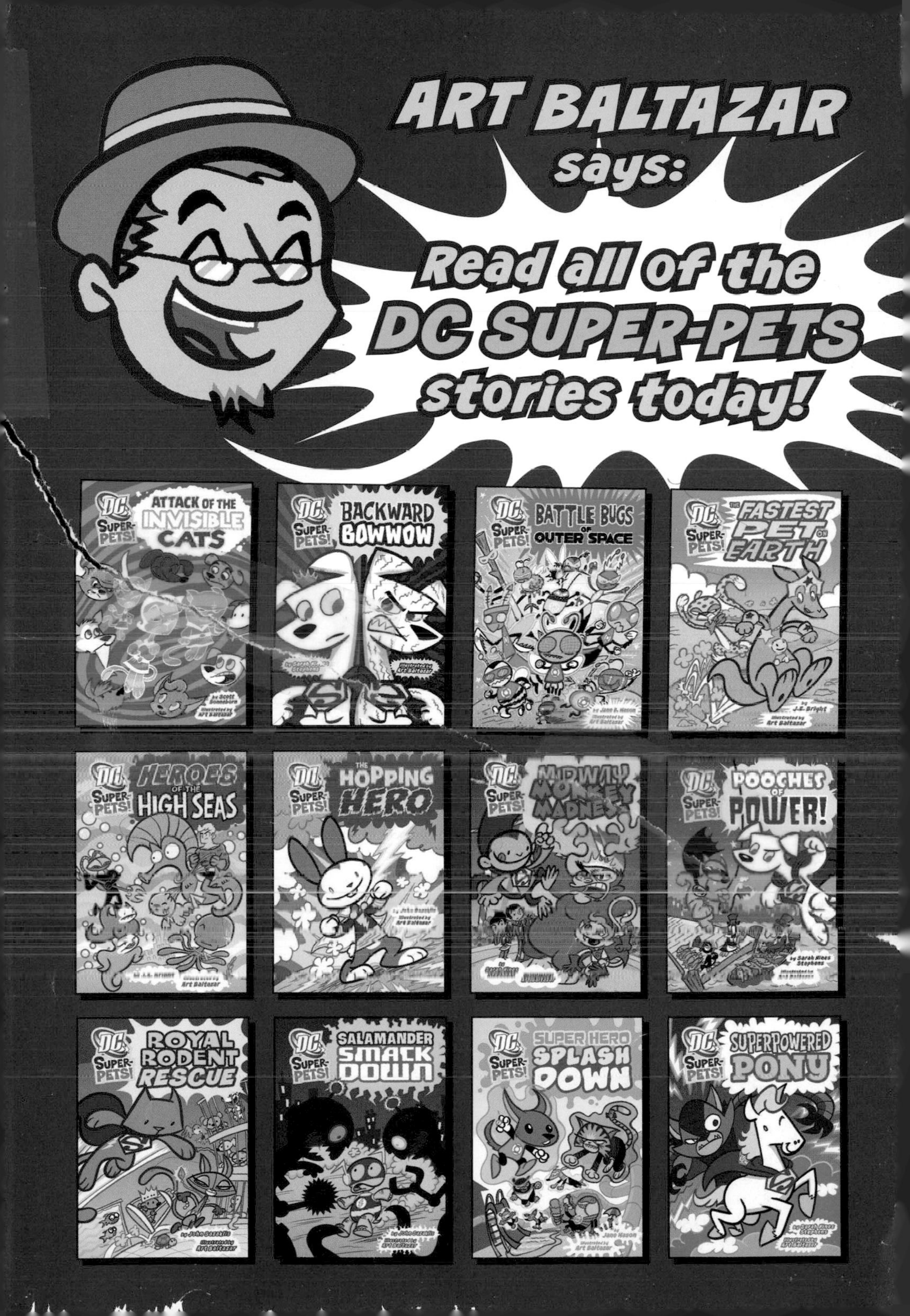
ART BALTAZAR
says:
Read all of the
DC SUPER-PETS
stories today!
ATTACK OF THE INVISIBLE CATS
BACKWARD BOWWOW
BATTLE BUGS OF OUTER SPACE
THE FASTEST PET ON EARTH
by J.E. Bright
Illustrated by Art Baltazar
HEROES OF THE HIGH SEAS
Art Baltazar
THE HOPPING HERO
MIDWAY MONKEY MADNESS
POOCHES OF POWER!
by Sarah Hines Stephens
ROYAL RODENT RESCUE
by John Sazaklis
Illustrated by Art Baltazar
SALAMANDER SMACKDOWN
SUPER HERO SPLASH DOWN
Jane Mason
Illustrated by Art Baltazar
SUPERPOWERED PONY

Picture Window Books™

Published in 2012
A Capstone Imprint
1710 Roe Crest Drive
North Mankato, Minnesota 56003
www.capstonepub.com

Cataloging-in-Publication Data is available
at the Library of Congress website.
ISBN: 978-1-4048-6478-8 (library binding)
ISBN: 978-1-4048-6844-1 (paperback)

Summary: When two naughty newts escape
from a pet store, nothing can stop their
amphibian antics — except the Terrific
Whatzit! This super-speedy turtle must stop
the slimy salamanders before they cast
another tale of terror on Central City.

Art Director & Designer: Bob Lentz
Editor: Donald Lemke
Creative Director: Heather Kindseth
Editorial Director: Michael Dahl

Printed in the United States of America
in North Mankato, Minnesota.
052012   006768R